P9-CFW-019

This **Monkey & Cake** book
belongs to:

Gadiel Tolentino

To Soc & Flora –D.D.

My technique is a mix of dark pencils and acrylic. I use watercolor brushes with marten hairs and paper with no grain, usually Sennelier or Arches 300g. For my characters, I spend time observing attitudes and how children move, talk, and dance.

–Olivier Tallec

Text copyright © 2019 by Drew Daywalt
Illustrations copyright © 2019 by Olivier Tallec

All rights reserved. Published by Orchard Books, an imprint of Scholastic Inc., *Publishers since 1920.* ORCHARD BOOKS and design are registered trademarks of Watts Publishing Group, Ltd., used under license. SCHOLASTIC and associated logos are trademarks and/or registered trademarks of Scholastic Inc. • The publisher does not have any control over and does not assume any responsibility for author or third-party websites or their content. •
No part of this publication may be reproduced, stored in a retrieval system, or transmitted in any form or by any means, electronic, mechanical, photocopying, recording, or otherwise, without written permission of the publisher. For information regarding permission, write to Scholastic Inc., Attention: Permissions Department, 557 Broadway, New York, NY 10012. • This book is a work of fiction. Names, characters, places, and incidents are either the product of the author's imagination or are used fictitiously, and any resemblance to actual persons, living or dead, business establishments, events, or locales is entirely coincidental.
Library of Congress Cataloging-in-Publication Data available
ISBN 978-1-338-14390-4

10 9 8 7 6 5 4 3 2 1 • 19 20 21 22 23
Printed in China   62
First edition, April 2019
The text type and the display type was set in Burbank. • Book design by Jess Tice-Gilbert

a **Monkey & Cake** book

This Is MY Fort!

Written by **Drew Daywalt** • Illustrated by **Olivier Tallec**

Orchard Books
New York
An Imprint of Scholastic Inc.

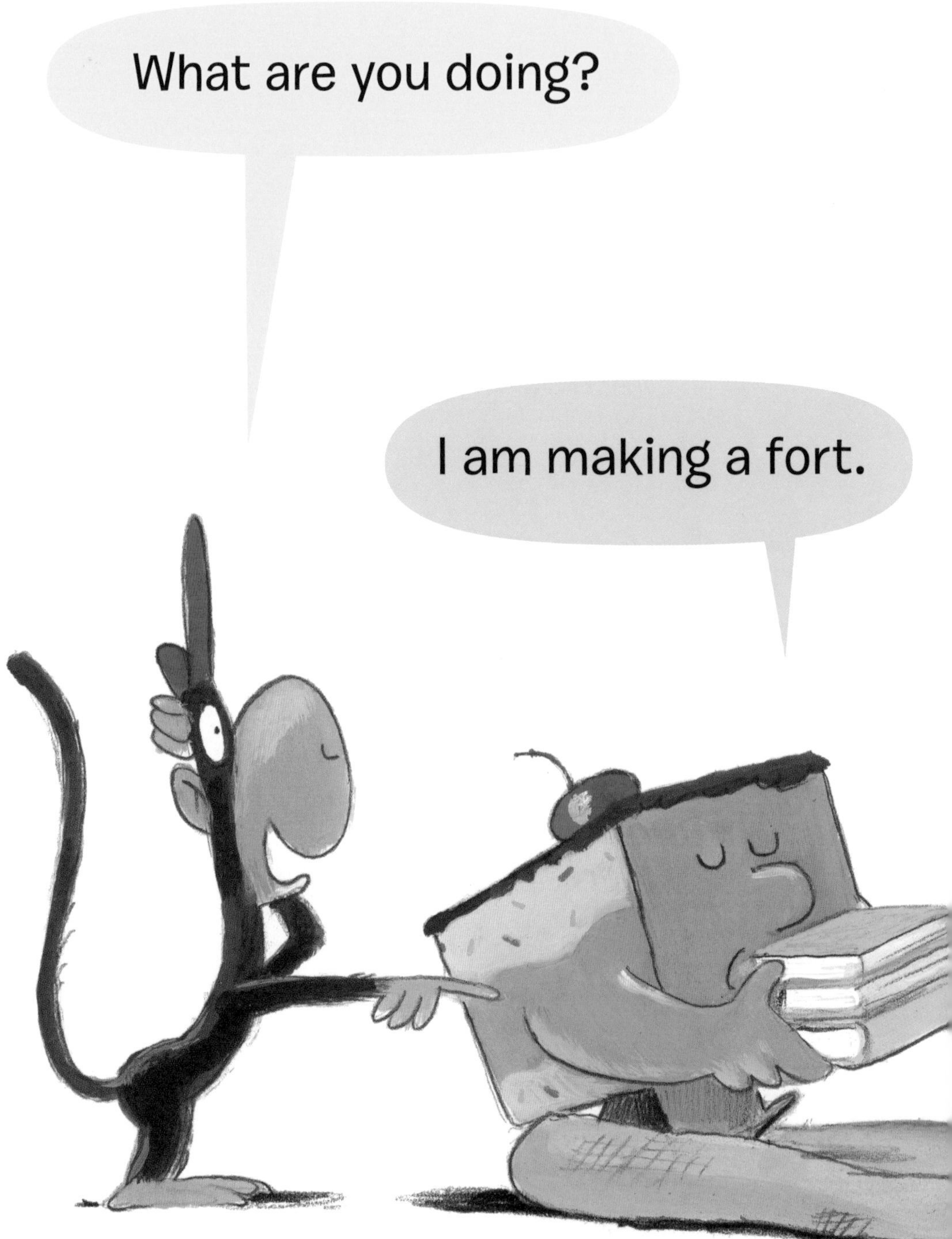
What are you doing?
I am making a fort.

I am making a fort to keep out Monkeys.
No Monkeys are allowed in my fort.

And I like forts.

I am a Monkey and
I want in the fort.

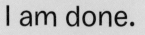

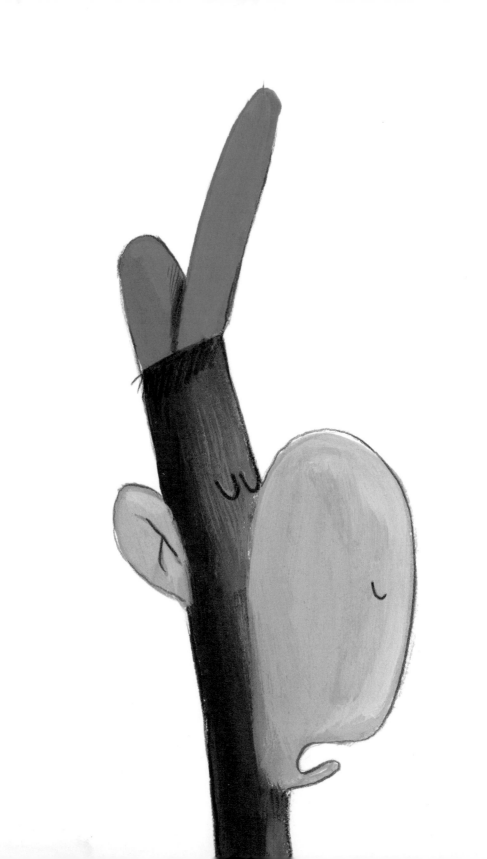

Good!

Then I am done, too.

I am done making **MY** fort.

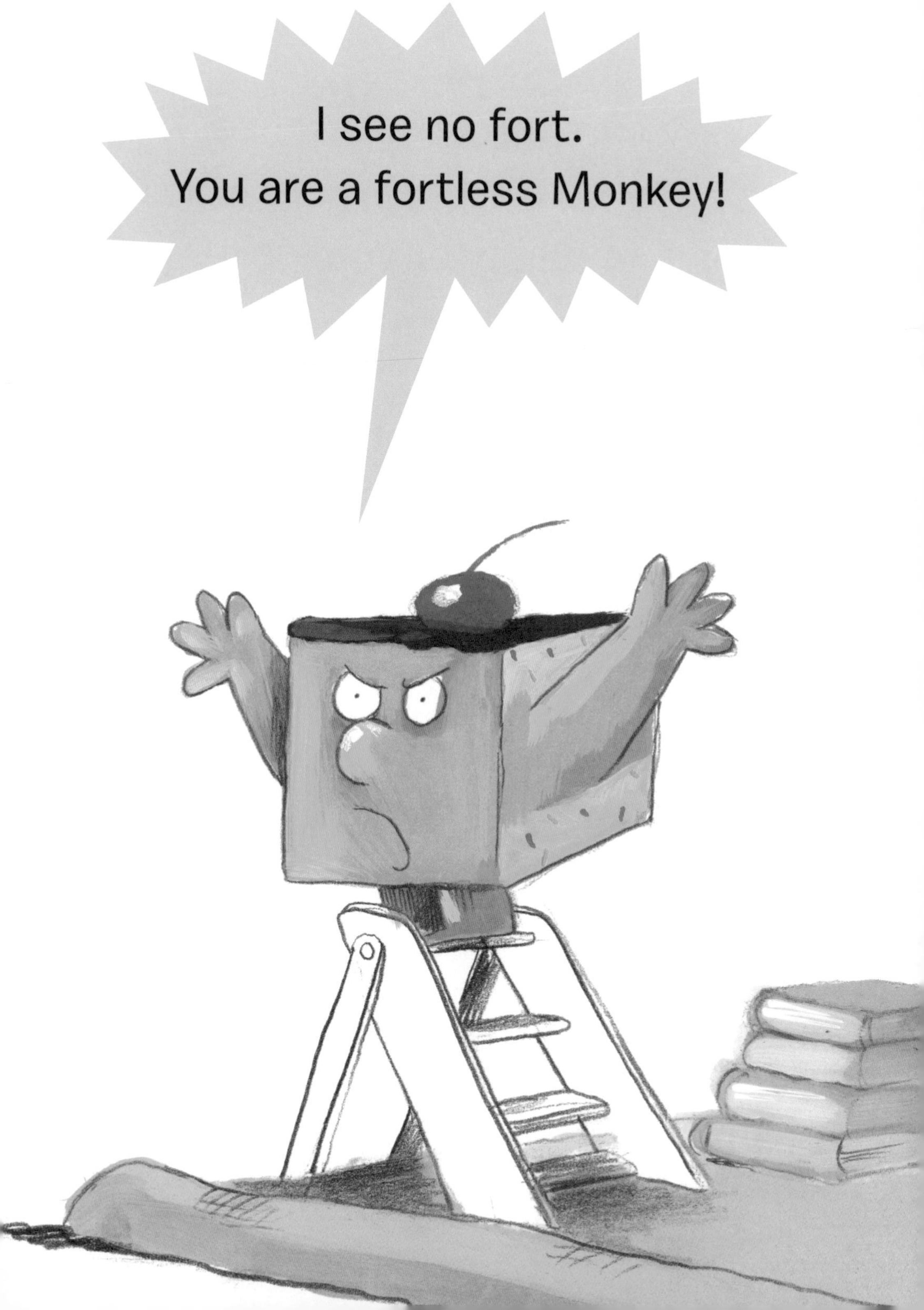
I see no fort.
You are a fortless Monkey!

I am a fortfull Monkey.
My fort is the whole world
except for your fort.

See the wall?

The wall to your little fort
is also the wall to my
"rest of the world" fort.

Oh yes!
My fort is big.
It is huge.
It is the whole rest of the world and your fort is small.

Hmm . . . My fort **IS** small.

Your fort is a trap!

OH YES!

I want to be out of my fort and in your fort!

You cannot come into my fort.
There are no Cakes allowed.

No Cakes are allowed in your fort?

No.

No.
This is a no-Cake fort.
Only Monkeys are allowed in this fort. I built this fort for no Cakes to be in it. Just Monkeys.